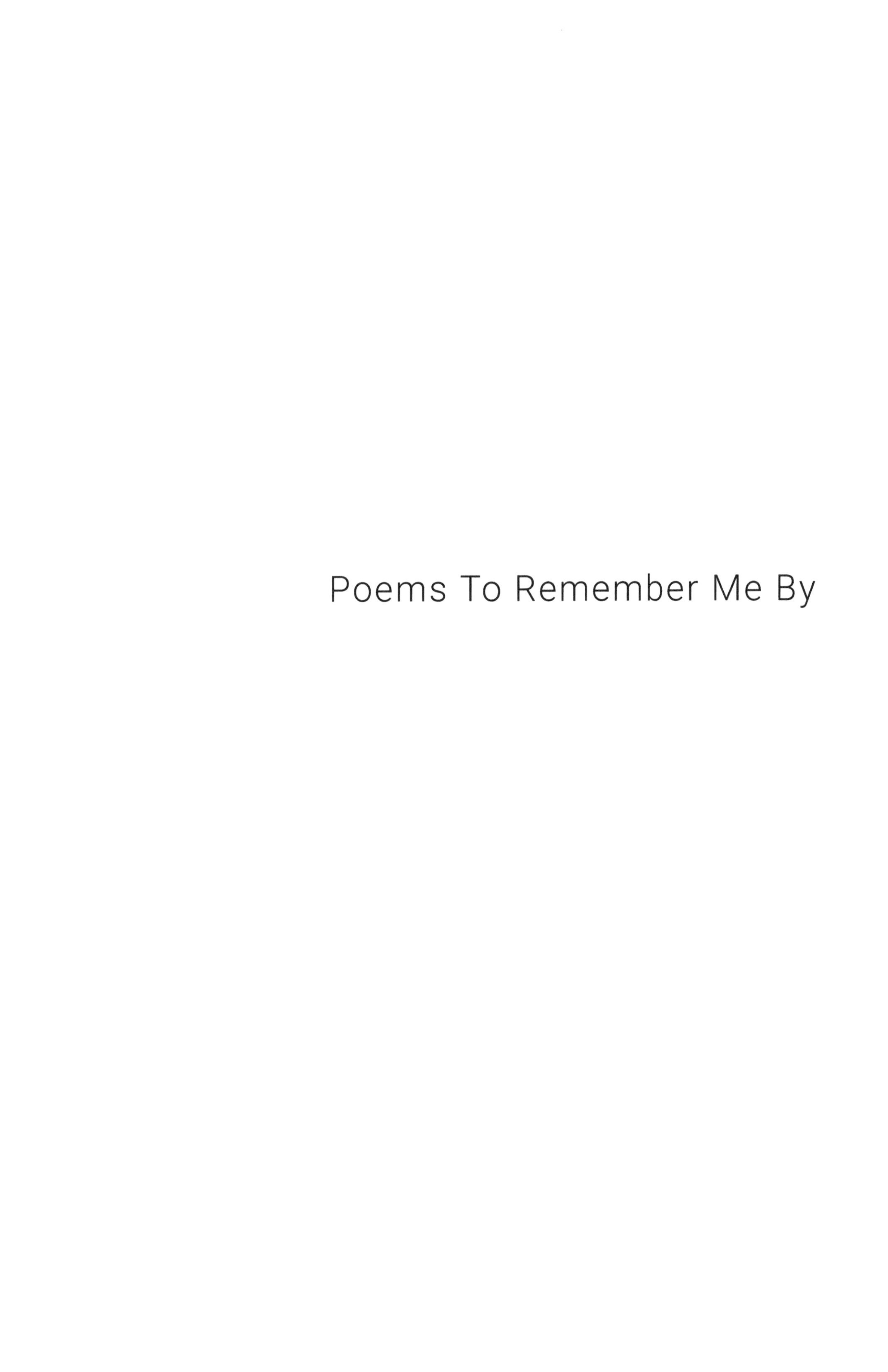

Poems To Remember Me By

Poems To Remember Me By

Justin A Guerra

Justin A Guerra

First and Foremost this book is dedicated to Carlee

Secondly, it is dedicated to all my girls who I love so much!

Table of Contents

Introduction

I often get looks of surprise when I tell people that I write poetry. Writing in general, and the writing of poetry in particular, has become less common in our modern world. Many people today might "write" but in short bursts such as text messages, tweets, or quick responses to a post on social media. However, the art of truly writing something of substance, a story, an essay, or a poem, is just not something most people do any more. In our society reading poetry isn't something people do much of either. I think this is a great tragedy for our society and our children.

The reading and writing of poetry can have profound effects on the development of a society, how we learn, what we appreciate, and our ability to communicate in an artistic yet meaningful way. When we look at the past, we can see the use of poetry in almost every society that has a written language. The ancients used poetry to pass on their history. The religions of the world use poetry to teach life lessons. Poets like Langston Hughes and Claude McKay used poetry to fight injustice.

Poetry is unique in its ability to speak to our heart and soul. The only other thing like it would be a song, but I would argue this is just another form of poetry. A poem's ability to speak to life's great pains and sufferings, life's greatest joys, or share timeless wisdom is unmatched. Poetry has an ability to speak to our hearts and souls through the rhythm of verse that takes us to the core of our being and resonates on a level so natural and primal that it's hard for us to really explain.

Unlike having to read a long essay or novel though, a poem's ability to do all this in typically a short form is incredible. Poetry can tell stories; our story, the story of others. It can bridge gaps and open us up to new worlds like we have never seen before. It can inspire us to take action or stop us in our tracks. The power of poetry is unmatched in the world of literature. This is why it makes me sad to see its demise in our modern time.

Poetry has always been a part of my life and I try to make
it a part of my children's lives as well. I write them poems,
each Valentine's Day for example. We read poetry together.
We will set a time where we all go and grab a book of poetry
that we like best. Then we take turns reading poems out loud
to each other. It's a great way to spend time together, to laugh
and cry and learn together, and to create memories together.
I hope your family might start this as well, and I hope this book
might be an option to share.

The poems in this book I wrote for a variety of reasons.
Some to entertain my children. Some to tell them how much
I love them. Some I wrote for my wife to tell her how I feel.
Others I wrote for other family members. I wrote some because
I thought of a funny idea. Some to share a point or piece of wisdom that I felt was best
communicated in the form of a poem. Others I wrote just because I had to get an idea out of
my head. Nonetheless they were all written to be read, and many to be read out loud.

The poems vary in topic, some are about nature or animals, my family and I like to spend a lot
of time in nature and observing animals. Some are about traveling or going on adventures,
which we also like to do. Others are simply funny because it's fun to let randomness have a
little bit of your day too. Not every poem will speak to you, but I hope as you read through
them you might find a few that do.

In the end I hope these poems will touch you in some way. That they make you laugh or cry,
that they make you think, or view the world differently. I wish they will make you want to read
more poetry, and may I dare to wish that they may inspire you to want to write a poem of your
own. I hope you find them entertaining but meaningful. I hope you share them with others,
and that they bring people together. Most of all, I hope they can inspire you in some way or
help you in some way wherever they may find you.

So let's journey together
Let's jump in and give it a try
Who knows what we might find, what treasure
Or what awaits in these poems to remember me by

Justin A. Guerra

Invitation

If you like fancy things
Things so nice and new
If you like your world in order
Without a problem or a hitch to work through
If you fear the abstract
The crazy, silly, and unknown
If you'd rather stay safe
While sipping tea on Sunday afternoon
THEN STAY OUT! YOU'VE BEEN WARNED!

But if you like the unexpected
And thirst for an unusual show
If you like the journey of adventure
More than the destination so
If you think this world wrong
But want to make it right
If you want to laugh and roll and make your side hurt
Then proceed on, let your imagination take flight
But you too should tread with care
For you know not what may come or from where…

Adventure

Adventure is something that everyone will experience in life. Some with a higher level of enthusiasm and others with less. Some will seek it out and others will seek to avoid it. Yet, I would argue that adventure is one of the great spices of life. I would encourage you to seek and enjoy adventure wherever it can be found. Whether that be trekking through the African bush, floating along the flooded forest in the Amazon, wandering through the beauty of a local national park or taking in the birds and plants in one's own backyard. You could even enjoy a great and wonderful adventure within the imagination of your mind. No matter where, how, or when, the benefits are great nonetheless. If you are so inclined then, please come join me as we embark on adventure.

Alone At Sea

To fear and struggle all alone at sea
A life full of everything except for me
An old soul is often said I am
Yet still as young as the sacrificial lamb

I'm tired and full of life's contradictions
To be old of young is quite an odd condition
I know… but unable to share
Never shall I leave my breast bare

This risk so fleeting high
Is all it takes to be by and bye

How blessed and cursed I may be
To live in the universe you can't see
That's the life and truth of me
To be out and stranded alone at sea

Pirate Adventures

I always thought it would be fun
To be a pirate out at sea
To sail under the ocean sun
With my first mate Smee

We'd have great adventures
Taking treasure from Kings and ships
Giving the slip to the jailer
As I slid through their fingertips

We'd visit faraway places
See deserted islands and beaches of endless sand
Riding the waves up and down, up and down, putting our face to the ocean breezes…
Now I'm wishing for land

I know I get sea sick
Why'd I think being a pirate would be terrific
I can feel my stomach twirl
Here it comes, I have to hurl

Troll

They says we are big, fat, and dumb
They makes fun of us and kicks our bum
They talk about our terrible teeth
And the nasty smells we bequeath
They're always making funs of how slow we are
That we can'st travel so far
I just don'ts get why they haves to be so mean
Don'st they remembers how hard it was at fourteen
At least I'm not afraidst of the dark
(Although that sun is as scary as a shark)
What I wouldst really like is to make amends
Can'st we just be friends?

Fairies in my Yard

There are fairies in my yard
This I am sure
I have seen their light flicker
That's what put me on guard

But they fly so fast
I can't ever get a good look
Although I hear them buzz
By my ear when they fly past

On warm summer nights
As I listen from my window
I can hear their song
Floating on the breeze's heights

This music so sweet I keep
As I lay my head to sleep

The Far Darrig's Tree

As I wandered through the forest
Of huge hemlocks and old oaks
I happened upon a queer tree
Its trunk was large and bumpy
It's bark was thick and rough
The branches were gnarled and full of leaves
And it radiated magic, I don't know why
But as soon as I touched it
I flew into the sky
Then I heard a wee voice
Low and rough it said, "Who are you?"
I stammered "I'm little Michael Drew"
The wee voice asked another
"Why are you bothering me?"
I sputtered "mis..mistake, will you please let me free?"
The voice said "only if you leave me be"
I replied "I'd be happy to, I'd be much relieved"
Down I went to the ground, hard and fast
But curiosity got the best of me, so I asked
"Who are you?"
I looked around to see what I could see
Was the voice coming from the tree?
No, up high on the trunk
I saw a little door
In that little door stood a little man, a far darrig
As red and black as his magic
But as soon as we locked eyes
I knew he had got his prize

Hobbits

They live in a land that is lush
Green grassy hills rolling across the landscape
Under ancient trees and alongside fresh flowing streams
Their homes they dig into those grassy hills
So they don't disrupt the simplicity and beauty of the landscape

Their doors are round and hinged, of simple wood
Being a simple folk, they spend their time
Farming, eating and socializing about farming and eating
Being a short folk, only three feet tall
They are oft overlooked, like many a child

Yet the Hobbit prefers this, to go unnoticed that is
With unkempt brown or blonde hair
Simple but brightly colored clothes
Alongside their round and joyful faces
You always feel a simple joy being around them

Although they prefer to live a simple uneventful life
There are a few famous ones of note in history
Who went on amazing adventures
To dragon laid mountains in search of the treasure of dwarves
Or through the mystic land of the elves
Two went to a cave in a mountain full of bubbling lava and fire
(it's said they saved the world)

Although they are not incredibly strong
Nor are they expert with the sword or bow
They are extremely loyal, which is a trait
That should not be underestimated
They are also incredibly silent
And can sneak without being noticed
So they still can be quite useful

If you ever find yourself in the land of the Shire
I am sure you will see the charm of these folk
So grab a pipe and take a seat at their table
And soak in the simplicity of the Hobbit life
I am sure you will find it to be much agreeable
Who knows, you may just never leave

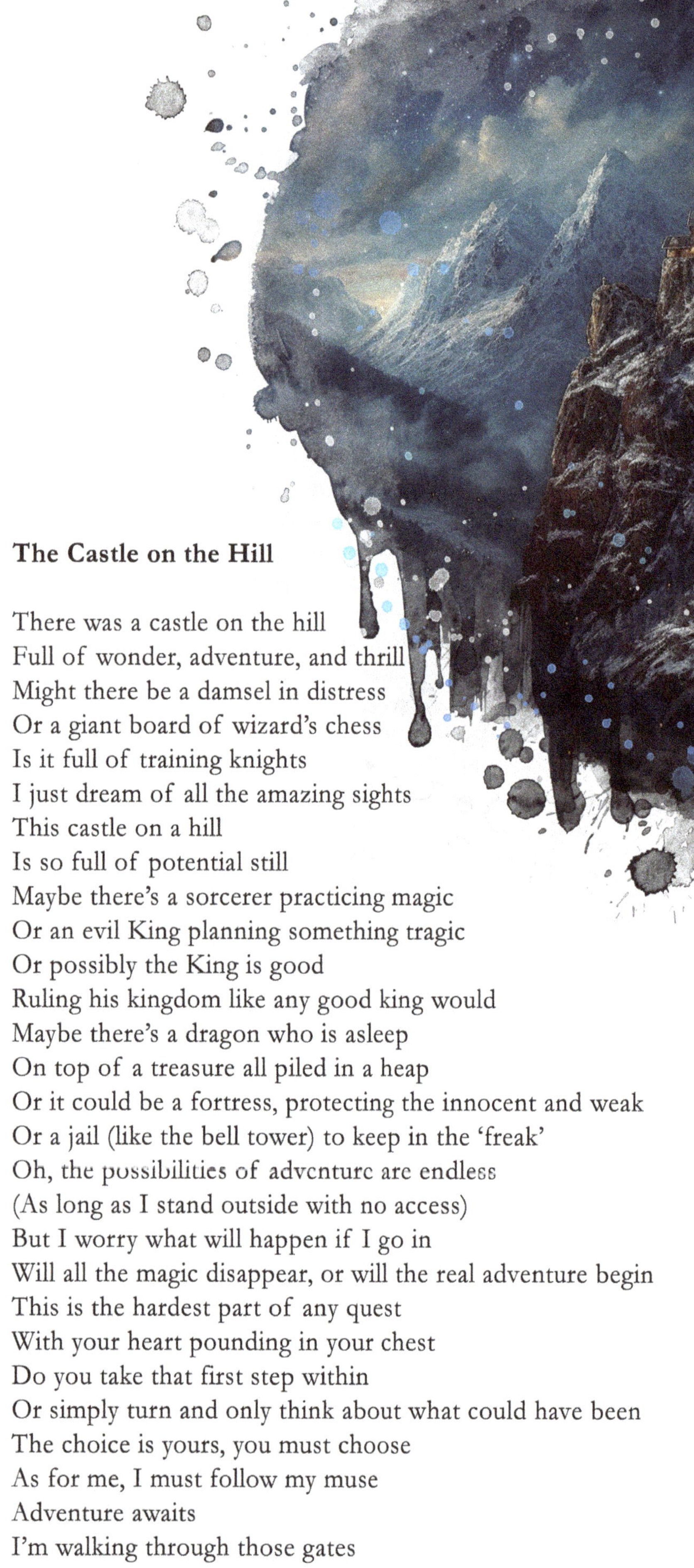

The Castle on the Hill

There was a castle on the hill
Full of wonder, adventure, and thrill
Might there be a damsel in distress
Or a giant board of wizard's chess
Is it full of training knights
I just dream of all the amazing sights
This castle on a hill
Is so full of potential still
Maybe there's a sorcerer practicing magic
Or an evil King planning something tragic
Or possibly the King is good
Ruling his kingdom like any good king would
Maybe there's a dragon who is asleep
On top of a treasure all piled in a heap
Or it could be a fortress, protecting the innocent and weak
Or a jail (like the bell tower) to keep in the 'freak'
Oh, the possibilities of adventure are endless
(As long as I stand outside with no access)
But I worry what will happen if I go in
Will all the magic disappear, or will the real adventure begin
This is the hardest part of any quest
With your heart pounding in your chest
Do you take that first step within
Or simply turn and only think about what could have been
The choice is yours, you must choose
As for me, I must follow my muse
Adventure awaits
I'm walking through those gates

Through the Night at Sea

Upon the boat with sails high
Out at sea where not even a bird shall fly
But the wind doth roar
And waves upon the deck shall pour
Through the night at sea

The boat does bounce upon the ocean
The rocking cradle, seamen doth sleep upon the motion
Until morning comes, bringing the rising sun in east
The battle raged with nothing to fight such a beast
Against such cunning and strength is the sea
But that's the dream and life of sailors like me

Stone Submarine

I made a submarine out of stone
To take me far away from the sandy shore
Just as I designed it, it sank to the bottom ocean floor
But I never thought about how to get back to the surface
I've seen the bottom and now I live with the fishes
Maybe a submarine of stone was foolish

Adventure

I may not have seen the terror of war
Or walked the streets of poverty
I may not be the bearer of medals
Or stand with the formal honors of civilization

But I have traversed across the lands of Africa
I have trekked through the jungles of Asia
I have touched the grand ice in Antarctica
I have traveled the outback in Australia
I have trudged through the wilderness of North America
I have trapezed across the treetops of South America
And I have tarried around the Europe of past Ages

To have sat upon the world's top
To have stood upon the world's bottom
To have sailed upon the world's oceans
To have seen it in all its wonderous beauty
I have surely lived to experience it in all its glory
Under the sunlight of day
Under the starlight of night

It's a life well-traveled
It's a life well lived
For I have gazed upon the foundations of our world
And I have been given the gift of adventure

A Swing

Gliding through the air
So smooth yet so swift
The breeze brushes through my hair
And tickles my stomach, what a joy, what a gift

Sometimes I'm an astronaut in space
Zooming through the Milky Way
Other times I'm an airplane ace
In a dogfight over a bay

I have been on a hang glider high in the sky
Soaring over cliffs and sea
Or a helicopter pilot secret spy
Looking for the stolen diamond tree

There really is no limit
To where I can fly
It is but a minute
You should give it a try

Inside Out

It's an odd world we live in
An odd world indeed
Where things seem so simple
But they are really as complex as can be

The world seems flat
Yet it is round like a ball
When I eat chili (salsa) at the restaurant
It's hotter than hot not cold at all

The grownups always tell me
To do what they say
But they don't even listen
Just watch as they do what they may

It seems so odd to me
That the happy memories
Can make you blue later when they are remembered

Yet there are others
That start sad in the darkest of mood
Although at the end we still find joy

This world is so confusing
I don't know what to do
I guess that's what makes life so interesting
Looking inside of you

For the Win

I was on the breakaway call
It was just me and the goalie
Nothing between us but the grass and ball
It seemed like time was moving slowly

I kicked the ball high and to the right
She lunged with her hands out
It seemed like she took flight
Then the crowd began to shout

The match was out of time
Man was that goal sublime

Down by One in the 9th with Two Outs and One On

I stand in the box
With the game on the line
Just waiting like a tinderbox
To blow like a mine

The crowd screams and shouts
In anticipation of the pitch
And my heads full of doubts
This fear I have to ditch

The crowd no longer makes a sound
Either in reality or just in my head
I don't even hear my heart pound
I'm in the zone, ready to put this to bed

My hands grip the bat
And my hips load the charge
A fastball down the middle, I anticipated that
Then the CRACK of the bat! Like a bomb discharge

Did I get a hit?
Did I score the run?
You'll forever wonder of it
Either way the game was done

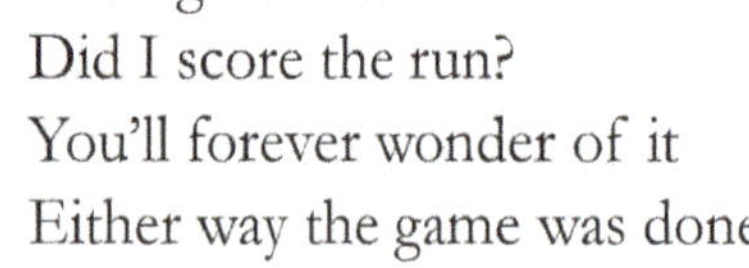

A Piano

The shadow is not shining
It was not respected
There was no arrangement to be played

Burnt and behind
Explaining darkness
Stands and feeds and silences

A little sign of an entrance
There is a disturbance
Yet more silence

Then thunder
There is music, harmony in hesitation
So nice and sweet

It was done
Music was in the air
This is a sound so natural

So the tune which is there has a little piece to play
It is not in a vision, but in the sound, that truth has come
This made the memory clear

No suggestion of silence
Music pleasing all
So triumphant

It plays a line in life
It is beautiful, this truth
Almost a religion

In ancient, success
Others question, in note it answers
The time was not so difficult

Being right is more than perfect
The sounds make sunshine
No song is sad

Music streams like a fountain
Magnificent, incredible virtue
-

Yet silence, -   again
-
-

Silence
-
-

Strange
-
-

Does silence choke music or does it not
No, -   sensible silence
-                     Separate attention

The Protector

Out of the night or in the middle of day
I am called to serve
In this my heart and law I must obey
That I might bring justice and judgement they well deserve

In the eyes of the public
Some friend, many a foe
But I swore to protect the republic
To do my duty I will go

Regardless of what public opinion may breed
My jobs to keep the order and uphold the law
This I swore, this is my creed
Upon this my strength I will draw

Beyond the wrath and tears
I will pursue the villain into the dark
There is nothing that I fear
And I always hit my mark

Sworn in as an officer in pursuit of peace
When in need you can count on me
Your humble servant who will never cease
To keep our neighborhood safe and free

Camouflage Christmas

I was deployed to a desert
Full of sand and dirt
I was called to my duty
To leave this land of beauty
Even though it's hard to go away
I could not have stayed
It's what my country needs
I will follow this path wherever it leads

From my family I have been taken away
To protect the world as it goes astray
Like Jesus, I will make the sacrifice
To do what's right, I never think twice
Although some of us may stay behind
Immediately to St. Michael's army they are assigned
To the oppressed, freedom we will bring
Just like the baby in the manager, our King

Sitting in the mess hall listening to the radio band
Dreaming of my family and Christmas so grand
Imagining my kids smiles on Christmas day
I wish there was another way
But if you asked me to do it again
I wouldn't hesitate or complain
Even if it's a one-way ticket
Sarg. put me in the thicket!

If a camouflage Christmas is what must be
As a soldier it's my job to protect the weak, then I agree
To go is really not choice
There are too many in the world without a voice
So, I must heed the call
To ensure peace and freedom for all

Dragons in the Deep

We can come with fire or ice
We are feared from the east to the west

Found in the deep
Deep below the waves of the sea
Deep below in the granite caves of the earth
Deep in the mountains amongst unknown valleys

Hidden
Simply looking for peace and solitude

As the sun sets
You may also see us high
Riding the wind above the clouds in the sky
Soaking up the sunset rays of red and orange

You shiver when we call
That shriek to ours
With a sound that creates terror
But the call is not of aggression
Not a call to war or vengeance

It's only the song of the dragon
Telling of times past
Our struggles and our triumphs
Of histories forgotten
Wisdom unknown to the 'intelligent' world

Understanding given to us to protect
In these hearts of gold
Underneath these scales of impenetrable armor

We could no longer co-exist
With the irrational fear of man
So, we dig deeper and fly higher

We went into hiding
To perpetuate the story of our extinction
To rise up above reality
To dig deep into the safety of myth

Where we will continue to reside
Continuing to preserve our past
Continuing to fortify our future

This is the call
Of the dragons in the deep

Phoenix

From ash to ash
With death I am resurrected
An ever-burning flame
Bringing light to dark places

A bird of fire
Who will induce cupellation in man's soul
All will bow when I take flight
To see my broad wings full and ablaze

I will change your immortal soul
An inferno feared by the wicked
But brilliant light of comfort
To those lost in the night

One drop of my tears
Can heal any physical woe
I bring confidence and hope
I am wonder and peace

A phoenix of fire and glory

The Warrior and the Drum

boom
boom ba boom
The drum of the warrior sounds
boom
boom ba Boom
The drum awakens the soul to life
Boom
It's the heartbeat, it's the call
Boom ba boom Boom

I am the Brave
Boom
Of the American Plains
Boom
I will fight for my tribe
Boom ba Boom
To protect our way of life
Boom ba Boom Boom

I am the Tequina
Boom
Who comes from the subtropics of an ancient world
Boom
I will fight for the tlatoani
Boom ba Boom
To gain prestige and wealth
Boom ba Boom BOOM

I am the Viking
Boom
Who rides upon the open seas
Boom
I will fight for me
Boom ba boom
To gather riches and prove my bravery
Boom ba BOOM BOOM

I am the Morani
Boom
One who has wrestled with lions
Boom
I will fight for the chieftain
Boom ba Boom
To protect our lands
Boom BA BOOM BOOM

I am the Ghazis
Boom
Who rides out from the Arabian sands
Boom
I will fight for the prophet
Boom ba BOOM
To bring respect to my religion
BOOM BA BOOM BOOM

I am the Nacoms
Boom
Who rises from the rainforest of life
Boom
I will fight for the gods
Boom BA BOOM
To ensure their protection of my people
BOOM BA BOOM BOOM

I am the Knight
Boom
From the round table
Boom
I will fight for my king
BOOM BA BOOM
To bring peace to the Kingdom
BOOM BA BOOM BOOM

I am the Samurai
Boom
Who comes from the misty mountains
BOOM
I will fight for the emperor
BOOM BA BOOM
To bring honor to my family
BOOM BA BOOM BOOM

I am the Soldier
BOOM
Who comes by tank, boat or plane
BOOM
I will fight for my country
BOOM BA BOOM
To defend freedom and protect the innocent
BOOM BA BOOM Boom

I am the Crusader
BOOM
Who comes from the Light
BOOM
I will fight the good fight for God
BOOM BA Boom
To bring truth and goodness to all mankind
BOOM Ba Boom Boom

I am a warrior
Boom Ba Boom Boom
I fight for a cause
Boom Ba boom
I fight for the fallen
Boom ba boom
I fight for the weak
boom
I fight for peace
boom
boom
boom ba boom …boom

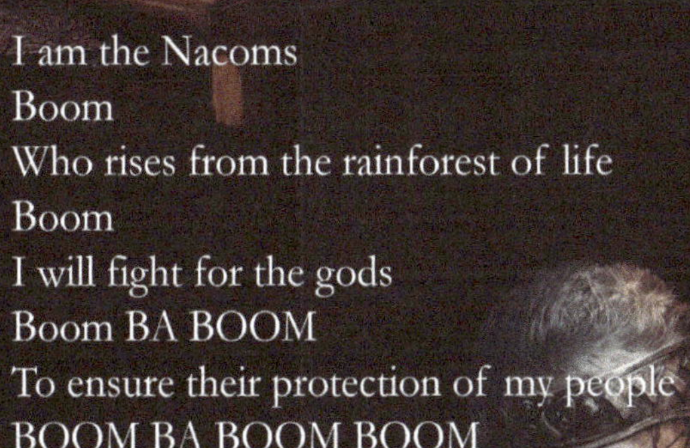

Alone Amongst Ruins

I awoke, or still asleep, it seemed
A barren place of sand I dreamed
The sun was high
Well up into the sky
But the ground was dark
The sand cool and stark
Wense appeared a man
Who wasn't there upon the horizon at last scan
Tall and sleek if a bit gray
Presented himself as Past who could not stay
Then another man appeared
A little fatter and with a beard
Who never really made it to us
But said his name was Future thus
I didn't notice before
But now we stood amongst ruins at the precipice of a door
Past encouraged me to go through
Future also calling me too
What's their aim I do not know
But my movements are hesitant and slow
Past shows me with perfect vision
Urging me to make a decision
Future promises me grand rewards
If only to the door I'd move towards

I ask Past to open my eyes
To show me things that will make me wise
I ask Future to show what may
He only replies to not delay
They show, or conceal, only what they wish me to see
But truly I wish to be free
So, I shout to them "depart from my sight"
Immediately their disappearance makes my soul light
For I wish to dwell in the here and now
Away from the burden of Past's plow
I wish to not fret about Future's unknown
For the knowledge of that belongs to God alone
But to stand here in the presence of the Present
I have found peace, I am content
Yet with the Present, Future and Past have become one
Experience, knowing this, now my education is done
I have found Heaven and the Way
Forever here I wish to stay
In this embrace in all time
Oh this dream, or now awake, is sublime

The Hunt

The stars in the sky above
Twinkle down upon the earth below
I sit in this darkness of
The beauty of the world we know

My gun slung upon my shoulder
As I traverse the landscape wild
I can feel the forest grow colder
At one with nature, we are finally reconciled

As I'm in pursuit of the prize
The beloved life I am to take
Yet some will question how I harmonize
This death with the love do I break?

No, it's truly love that drives me so
To protect this majestic wilderness
For this I want you to know
I am a conservationist

My love and respect are on par
With my awe of all God's creation
Whether an animal or a star
All were created by God's narration

So, with a seriousness and respect
I take this animals life for me
His purpose on earth I shall protect
For food his ancient ancestors were set free

When that rifle does fire
And that shot does ring
It's not the bloodthirst I desire
Rather I am honoring the life to which we all cling

For my shot is true
As the native in me always knew

This animal's sacred death
Through its meat shall bring sacred life
It's now fulfilled its purpose with this last breath
It won't even feel the cold sharpness of the knife

Space Explorer

Have you ever seen a sketch
Done in monochrome, black and white
I have, as I gazed upon clusters of galaxies
On a black slate where there is no night

Have you ever seen a sculpture
Molded in the hands of the creator
I have, as I marveled at the blown glass marbles we call planets
Shining by the light of their suns, there is no artist greater

Have you ever seen a structure
Crafted by the mind of the architect
I have, as I stood on the surface of alien worlds

Have you ever seen a watercolor
Done by the hand of God
I have, in the nebulas found in deep space
Brilliantly colored with laced nebulosity, I was awed

Have you ever seen a being
Born and loved into existence
I have, as I encountered flora and fauna that has never been seen
Some quite frightful but others with indescribable magnificence

But this is the state and privilege of my life
As an adventurer of space
For my job is to travel through the wide universe
Exploring for the human race

Fireworks

There's nothing like fireworks
Bursting on the fourth of July
Whether standing with a hotdog on a cul de sac
In the land of suburbia
Or in a park in the middle of a city
Whether sitting upon the edge
Of a lapping lake so serene
Or in a baseball stadium full of people
To see those sparks of red, white, and blue
Burst into flowering flames of man-made stars
To hear the pop of victory
Reminiscent of the bombs that brought this freedom
My heart swells with pride
How I long for such a summer night
So timeless now it seems
To hold a sparkler in your hand
Writing your name and waving it around
Like a flag of victory
Or to watch the flowers strobe upon the street
To the sound of ooh's and aah's
And the purity of laughter among the kids
Oh how I go back to better, simpler times
Each time I see a firework
Bursting on a hot and beautiful summer night
On the fourth of July

Memories

It's a funny thing, how memories work
Brought on by a word, a picture, a smell
It's a funny thing, these memories
Like little time machines, taking us to times past
Sometimes letting us drive, letting us go where we want
Sometimes they force us
Whether we want to follow them or not
There are times when we can even linger
Stand and live in that moment, frozen in time
More often though one leads to the next
In a rapid and logical sequence, many times not
They can be a wonderful thing, these memories
They can be a terrible thing, these flashes of the past
Like a mirage summarizing what has been
Like virtual reality letting me live what was
I can feel, I can feel what I felt
See what I saw, hear what I heard
Smell the scent as if they are here now
Reminding me of all I am, the sum of my life
The trick is to catch them, like a firefly in summer
Can you hold it, share it, let it be a light in the dark
They are what I was and explain who I am
Like diamonds of sparking light within me
These memories, these funny little, sometimes dreadful,
But mostly blessed and wholly mine, memories

Canvas

The written word is but a shadow of the original thought
So in a book wisdom cannot be found
If it's truth that is sought
Retreat to silence in your head, there should be no sound
Close your eyes, meditate
All thought in your mind eradicate
Slow your breath and open your heart
This is how to start
Then sit still and cleanse the soul
This is where you pay the toll
It's here that God's love will begin to cure
It's here the canvas is wiped blank, made pure
Upon this canvas He wills the paint
The beauty of truth, as with every saint
It's here we find complexities simple answer
After the fall our flesh, our mind, is cancer
In your soul endeavor to love but the One
Mimic all the ways of His Son
Let His Spirit burn in your heart
God and you will never again be apart
In this unison you can then know all
But try too hard to grasp it, it will fly away like the leaves of fall

Silly Part 1

Laughing, smiling, and having a generally fun time is a universal form of medicine that is often underused in today's age.   Unfortunately, when it is used it is often used in a manner that seems to be harsh and degrading to someone. So, we must try to avoid such endeavors while still being able to frolic in the revel and joy of clean and innocent fun, pun, and merriment that comes from the unexpected and randomness that is our expectations. Some of these poems are funny because they are just so random you will wonder where such thoughts came from. Others are funny because they take situations out of context. While others are funny but only to those who catch the subtly of the language and follow the clues to the hilarious end they may lead. If you are ready for some truly good fun, follow me to the silly part one.

Today, Tomorrow, or Yesterday

If tomorrow's yesterday is today
And if today is yesterday's tomorrow
But still yesterday's tomorrow is today
Is today's tomorrow yesterday?
Or is yesterday's today tomorrow?
Yet, still, it could be tomorrow's today yesterday.
I don't know, I thought it was *Thursday*

Nothing

They say nothing comes from nothing
But if nothing comes from nothing
Then something came from nothing
Nothing

If nothing is something
Then something did come from nothing
Even if they say nothing comes from nothing
Yet something did
Nothing

Well I can prove that something came from nothing
Because it was nothing that gave me this headache
A headache is something
Something that came from nothing

My headache is something
It certainly came from nothing
So, they are liars and my hurt head proves it
Now be quiet, I have a headache
But don't worry its nothing

Flower or Flour

How beautiful you are
Shinning of the purist white
You look so soft and smooth in that jar
Holding you in my hand you are so light

Oh how I need you so
As much as the florist, or is it the baker more?
Have you figured it out, do you know?
Is it a flower or flour that I yearn for

In my bread and the garden bed are both in need
In which I am responsible of only one indeed
Is it flour or a flower?
You decide and let me know by the hour

For there is work to be done
When you figure it out give me a shout
How I love the warmth of the sun
There's nothing like starting the morning with a fresh bun

Flour and Flowers
Gardens and Kitchens
Breads and Beds

What a sensation to smell
Aren't the aromas of life swell

Splash

So what if it rains
If the water falls or it pours
Let it wash away your pains
Put that umbrella back and head outdoors

Let's get all wet
Down to our drawers
The rain's really no threat
Just jump into that puddle of yours

Make a huge splash
Watch your happiness level
It will shoot up in a flash
With this rain, let's revel

Let's jump and let's dance
Through the puddles in the rain
Anytime I have the chance
I won't hesitate to jump in again

For these puddles are really nice
You don't have to ask me twice

My Favorite Star

Upon the stars I loved to gaze
To see their twinkle and their blaze
Upon my back in a meadow I lay
Looking at my favorite star by day
Then something utterly unexpected happened
The whole world went whitened
Then it all went blackened
Now I can't even see the stars of night
My mom warned me I would lose my sight
Who knew she'd be right?

Jack's Sack

There was once a boy named Jack
Who liked to run around with his sack
But one day he heard a whack, whack, whack
A whack, whack, whack coming from his sack
So he took his sack, right off his back, and put in on the haystack
And when he opened it up, right next to his cup, there sat a tiny little yak

The Old Man Greg

There once was an old man named Greg
Who's head was as bald as an egg
And when the sun shone down
    Upon his crown
He fell and broke his leg

Palm Tree

I am the palm tree
So thin and tall
Horizon to horizon, from sand to sea
I'm the best because I can see all

Big Blue Sea

I am the big blue sea
Such a vastly sprawl
Where sea life roams free
That's what makes me above all

Sandy Beach

I am the warm sandy beach you see
Broad or small, wonderful it is to be me
Where sailor and tourist do call
This is why I'm the greatest large or small

Tiny Crab

I am a tiny crab you will agree
But if there is anything I know at all
Is the palm, sea, and sand were made for me
As they are at my beck and call

For the sand shall warm my shell
And the sea will provide my food
Under the palm is where I dwell
So yes, they are all in my servitude

Fly

There was a fly who flew by the fly of a fly for this is how he flew
But one day he flew by a fly who knew not how to fly
So he was squashed to bits by a shoe

Little Duckies

One ducky, two ducky
Three ducky, four
All swimming around
Looking for some more

Onc looked up
One looked down
One looked
All the way around

All they could see
Was water and sky
So they all flapped their wings
And learned how to fly

Days Night

The sun's shining
With the moon smiling too
The days wailing
What's the night to do?

Red Button

I'm on a ship headed to space
Because my mom asked me to clean my room
I see this red button blinking in my face
I just can't remember if red is vroom…
Nope… its BOOM!

Why is Twinkle Hiding?

Twinkle twinkle little star
Why don't you sparkle where you are
With the sun so bright and high
Why can't I see you in the sky
Twinkle twinkle little star
Why don't you sparkle where you are

The People Upstairs

Have you heard the people upstairs on the top floor?
Aren't they just obnoxious and annoying?
They tap dance on the tile
And wrestle on the floor
They jump off the beds
And slam all the doors
When they watch movies
It's like the surround sound is in my room
And I swear they have a freight train
I hear the crash of pots and pans
They yell at each across the room
They snore like elephants
And sing loudly in the shower
What floor do I live on you ask?
Oh, I live on the top floor
The only rooms up there
The view is grand

Behind the Locked Door

Do you ever wonder
What your parents are doing
When they are behind that locked door
Inside their bedroom?

Well, I will tell you
They are throwing their clothes
All over the floor
And jumping on the bed

They have everything out of their closets
Scattered all over the room
As they run around and play
Doing all the things they told you not to do

Now you say "that's just not fair!"
"Why do they get to do those things?"
The difference is they pick it all up
So you would never know

Besides, when you are a parent
You will do those things too

Noodle Haiku

Sitting on a hill
Contemplating Yangtze River
Eating warm noodles

Great Wall

It is a great wall
Built to protect from foreigners
Ironically, now today
Brings millions to it

Fortune Cookie

Open fortune cookie
Sharing with friends brings smiles

Paper said you will laugh with friends
Now fortune is true

The Dark Corner

I was staring off into the sky's blue
As I sauntered curiously through my head
In the depth of space I saw time true
To the wisdom of knowledge and truth it read

All this I tucked away in a dark corner of my mind
To keep it safe and sound

I tucked it and experienced it…nothing like its kind
But like a dream chased away by the morning sun,
  where I left it I cannot find

Oh, how I feel to have what I had
But the slightest trick I don't
To the deepest depths I search, I'm sad
Yet quit the search I won't
Yet quit the search… I won't

The Prayer of a Snowman

As the sun begins to rise
I see those bright blue skies
I know the grass is green
So what can all this mean
Lord, please make it cold
So my snow pack will hold
On this bright day
In the middle of May
Amen

A Girl and Her Phone

There was a young girl on a hike
In a beautiful forest by the dike
She loved the outdoors and the trees
Her dad said "won't you look up please"
She replied "No, I have the view I like"

Nature

The natural world is a paradise that all humans should yearn for. It's where we came from and where we deep down long to return even if we don't know it. Like wildlife, the natural world around us was given to us to protect and be the stewards of, by God. It's in nature that we can enjoy so much of his creative work and where our souls can find rest and rejuvenation. However, to ensure that future generations will have natural places to enjoy and explore we must do a better job of protecting them now. I believe the first step in this endeavor is to help people recognize and connect with the environment around them. In this experience we can begin to reconnect with the natural beauty around us and in this reconnection our appreciation for and natural will to protect these spaces will grow. Let's go and immerse ourselves in the beauty we call nature.

The Beach

I look to the never-ending horizon
The sun sits low at this time of day
Then I step forward
My feet feel the cool sand run between my toes
The same sand that once scorched the feet
Of those it touched just a few hours ago
There's a cool breeze running
From the north to the south
That brushes by leaving chills along my spine
I breathe the crystal fresh air
I hear the serene sound of the waves
As they roll into the shore, then draw back to the sea
There is no one around
To the left, or to the right
This entire place is empty, calm, and at ease
The sun begins to set
Its radiant light reflects off the constantly moving sea
And runs through the depths of the sky
It spreads the colors of reds and yellows
Purples, oranges, and blues
These colors blend together
Creating natural art in the sky
As the sun begins to slowly fall beyond the earths edge
The temperature begins to drop
And the sky begins to darken
Stars appear in the night
Like millions of little diamonds spread across the sky
I take one final look at this miraculous sight
Then I turn to leave
With the image of this beautiful place
What I see as Heaven on Earth
Given by God's grace

Sunset

I look to the horizon
As the sun sets slowly to the west
I can see the increments of Heaven
As the suns rays infest
The darkening sky
With colors galore
As if it were the fourth of July
I can't help but to adore
The magnificent sight before my eyes
Such beautiful combinations of yellow and red
That the sun does comprise
The colors as warm as a child's bed
The sun dims into the night
As the moon now gives the light
I look to the broad and calm ocean
As the breeze comes in from the sea
The breeze gives a deep and meaningful sermon
A testimony to life and God's mercy
The waves also speak of a truth
A truth to love and your only one
Yes, the waves say to the youth
Covet thy life as the pure and simple virgin

From Up Above

Gliding through the air
Above the clouds so high
Looking out from a blanket of clouds
So soft, so white, fluffy and rolling
Down to earth, sprawling and green
Mother Earths an amazing thing
What hand, what mind, has master craft thee
With divine design from atom to galaxy
It is all the same, all different
It is all amazingly beautiful

Spring

Is it the spring or a spring you want
The sun shining and the flowers in bloom
Or rushing water under the glimmering moon

Is it the spring or spring you seek
The beginning of life, the cycle renew
Or the abundance of life, upon a drop of dew

Mother Earth

I go walking through the valley of life
There's no better time than after a night fall of rain
As the sun struggles to warm that cold November morning air
The sky's as blue azure as a Brazilian macaw
I see the white clouds as soft and light as whipped cream
The glow of the valley is as green as an innocent child
The mountains capped to the East with powder as pure and soft as flour
The waves of West roll in like the metronome of Mozart
As far as the eye can see to the true horizon as the earth crests to other times
It's amazing how efficient, clean, and powerful Mother Earth really is
To wash away all that unnatural, manmade destruction with such ease
A little rain, a small breeze, and She's as pure as the day we arrived

Supernova

I was once a star
Giant, radiant, and full of energy
I was born, and I lived
But as time moved forward
(As that's all it can do)
I realized that I can't just burn
Just burn for me or burn forever

No, it was my time to die
But when a star dies
We go out in style
I go all black
Then there's a burst
Of bright light
That's when I go all white

From the fireworks display
I die to myself
But the shock of my death
Sends forth life
As all the blocks of life
Are shared and radiate out
Sent out to the whole universe

Sent out to create life
Even human life
Yes, humans are
Made of star dust
Don't worry about me though
My spirt, called a nebula, lives on
Still watching over the universe

For those who head to the desert
Or climb to the top of the mountain
If you look up to the heavens
There my spirit still shines
In full color of all the rainbow
As a reminder to all
For those who seek will surly find

Star Gazing

I look up at the shimmer of the sky
Like sugar crystals spread across the blackboard
How curious it is to think
These lights are the same that Jesus saw
It's awesome to be able to see into the past
For their light is millions of light years old
Just think of the journey it made
Simply for my humble eye to behold
Just a glimmer or a glimpse of its light
Oh how beautiful is such a sight

In Spring it is the Dawn

In spring it is the dawn that makes the season. The way the night dew melts in the warm morning sun. The flowers rise from their slumber and the shadows are cast upon the green ground. With a light breeze the sweet scent of spring, refreshing the world.

In Summer it is the Night

In summer it is the night that all remember, when the sky is ruled by Scorpio and Leo. The stars shine brighter in the untainted dome of the black abyss. The warm air makes it comfortable to walk under the trees of green and listen to the summer breeze from the west talk to the summer breeze of the east. This is the time of baseball and friends and family vacations. Summer is unlike all the rest.

In Fall it is the Evening

Fall evening. This is a time of year unforgotten to all. With the winds in full force backed by the upcoming winter chill and the trees shed to the bone with a rustle of leaves that swirl upon the air. The sky grows dark with gray. The seasons color changes from green to orange, and yellow. With the harvest moon and apples abundant there's no season as great and beautiful as fall.

In Winter it is the Day

Winter after fall brings joy to the soul as the season becomes pure with the fresh lay of powder. Although natural life is unseen, nature is very much alive. The sun shines bright off the perfect snow. The winter temperature brings that sudden chill upon your spine. But winter is a time of warmth and family with the fireplaces blazing as smoke billows out of the chimney. The merry sound of love and thankfulness fills the season, which brings death and life as the season passes through the new year.

The Scent of a Rose

A smell so sweet
Tickled my nose
It was such a treat
From a pretty rose

My soul is light
And it changed my day
It's such a delight
I wish they would stay

Drop

How pure life can be
If only I were but a drop of water
On a leaf upon a bush or tree

Unmoved… untouched liquid free
Warm from the sun
Cool from winters brisk degree

So round and smooth a sea
The abundance of life
In a single drop of dew are thee

Double Star

What a trick you played on me
To make me think you're one
Not knowing that you're really two
How clever though am I
In my scope so keen
I can split you from one to two
Now I see both of you

All

All the worlds but a drop of rain
All knowledge is but a fleeting fall leaf
All love is but the calm of the bright harvest moon

And all wisdom is lost in a dream
But in the glorious light of the sun
They all become but one

Untitled #28

Desert morning so bright and clear
With the sun shining, the wind blowing, autumn is here
Days of warmth, nights of chill
With love we'll hope the seasons fill
For colors change as well as moods
The last bit of heat before the winters cool intrudes

Dusk

Sculptures adorn the cities
Frescos were painted from Michelangelo's sleeves
But the setting sun painting the western sky
Are prettier far than these

There are buildings that tower with bells that ring
As pretty as you please
But how the stars light up heaven, creating dancing lights upon the seas
In all the glory of God's design
Are still prettier far than these

I Remember the Clear Morning

I remember the clear morning when the sun awoke to the blue sky as the black of night followed
the moon in fright. It was upon this morning I smiled, for God gave me another day.

Light Pollution

How sad it is to look up at night
And see but a shadow of starlight
What of the Milky Way so bright
It's all light pollution that's my plight

Wanting to Play

All the girls and all the boys cry out that they want to play
For the spring rain has fallen, flowers are blooming in this the middle of May

This Morning

Laying there among the warm of my bed
With the cool air trickling through the window upon my head

The bird's songs flow through the air
Upon this morning so beautiful and fair

Simple Beauty

Watch cherry blossom
Beauty is simplicity
Float away on wind

The Calm

The calm
Smooth lips of the wind
Drew out the love within

Wisdom Haiku

Looking out to river
Over mountains and valleys
Silence finds wisdom

A River Runs Through

Throughout our lives we experience milestones through brief moments in time
But through time all is gone and lost, leaving us alone and scared
It leaves us living each day with nothing but memories of the past and endless hopes for the future
Like a flowing river running through, nothing remains the same

The Flower and the Bee

I sat watching a flower
So beautiful in the rain
When a bee came up
Looking for some nectar

I sat looking at a flower
So grand in the morning sun
When a bee flew away
With legs covered in pollen

I held a little flower
Fresh picked from the field
When a bee tried to smell it
Ouch! That hurt!

Seasonal Taste

Someone once asked, "what does summer taste like?"
I said sweet tea and watermelon down by the dike

"How about winter? What do you say?"
Hot chocolate and cookies to keep the cold away

"What about spring?"
Honeysuckle lemonade and strawberries are the thing

"How about autumn, with all those colors of fall?"
Apple cider and doughnuts for the best season of all

To Wake

I lie in bed, with the morning sun playing peak a boo with the moon over the mountain tops
I feel the cool breeze blow through the open window bringing the morning fog that separates the
      dream from wake
I hear the pecking of the woodpecker like the tapping of a branch on the house in the woods on a
      stormy night… yet it's spring outside
I smell the glory of the morning dew upon the grass and the dense flower fields, or it is the spray of
      the ocean mist as the Dawn Treader sails the seas
I taste the morning smoke from the fire that burnt the night away, where the wild things and I
      danced the dance of the wild all through the night
I see so much swirling around my head, at first as clear as the stars in the Oklahoma night sky, but as
      the hours, seconds, minutes, pass by… what was clear becomes hazy, what's hazy becomes foggy, what's
      foggy becomes nothing more than an inclination of what was
This inclination becomes nothing, for which the mind struggles to remember that which is
      unknowable in this conscious state
For, I lie in bed with the morning sun shining in through the open window, upon my sheets as I
      squint with confusions, ah day has come

Silver and Gold

Quiet
Slow and serene
Seasons shift and time sways
By the silver silence of the moon

Bright
Gradual yet grandiose
All growth is graciously given
By the great gold of the sun

Camping Deep in the Wilderness

The best alarm is lapping waves of a lake
As I drift between dream and wake
In the warmth of my bag in a tent
With wafts of pine and wildflower upon the airs scent

I step out into the warmth of the morning sun
I can't help but feel in the game of life I've won
To be in the old oak forest of serenity
Looking into the alpine meadow to the mountains is heavenly

To have watched the unhindered stars rise above the falls
And now to listen to the bird's songs and calls
For this is earths beauty unknown
Except to those who camp alone

Silly Part 2

Why are there two silly sections you ask? I would ask why not? Without the levity of the lighthearted we can often get bogged down with the serious. This is not to dismiss the serious, obviously you know if you read any of the other parts of this book there is plenty of serious. However, without the counterweight of the silly the mood can change too far. Rather I would like to keep a balance while keeping you on your toes. Now you have seen my sense of humor can be dark and dry at times, but it can also be a bit ridiculous. That's the great thing about funny, it can be different for different people, or for different moods, or for different times. Yet funny is still funny and it gives us the joy of laughter which is really like hearing angels sing. If you are ready for some more ridiculous, come… follow me.

OYGRB

beautiful Blue bravely boxes big boats boarded black
radiant Red remembers rambunctious radicals revealed ravishly ready
generous Green gratefully guides graceful gizzards grimly ground
yes, yummy Yellow yo-yo yarns yakked your yesterday
outrageous Orange opened optical ocean offices on octuesday

As Boring As Peas

The joys of pasts as sweet as the honey of bees
The excitement of futures as adventurous as sailing the seas
But the presents always as boring as eating peas

Writing a Haiku

Writing a haiku
Brings both fun and frustration
End brings joyfulness

Death of the Poem

To write a poem in one's head
Is as easy as apple pie
To put it to paper is its death
As the words disappear… why try

In the vastness of the mind
All clarity it comes together
From pen to tree the words I cannot find
Lost in my head forever

What genius, what wisdom I've lost
As leaves washed away in the rain
Oh how I have paid the cost
For all those poems I've slain

Nothing To Write

With nothing to write
I have nothing to say
Might as well turn out the light
Might as well put my pen to lay

In a Mirror

My whole world seems backwards
I don't know why
My whole life seems backwards
No matter how hard I try

Life would be so much easier
If I could live in a mirror
Then my view of the world
Would be the right way and clear

Reflection

Sometimes when I see that reflection
I laugh and make faces you see
How strange and funny this little is he
I always thought he was quite ridiculous
Until I learned that he is really me

Hug-O-War

Oh, what do I say
Oh, what do I do
When a boa constrictor wants to play
A game of hug-o-war with you

The Hat (Snake in Disguise)

If I were a snake and in need of disguise
I'd eat an elephant whole, from his tail to his eyes
Then they would all look, saying "What is that?"
"Oh, it's nothing, don't bother, it's just an old hat"

The Bells Rang

The bells ring all through the night
The sun has taken all of the light
My bed calls so quietly right
It awaits my soul, so soft and bright

The bells ring all through the night
I can no longer put up a fight
For darkness grows with all its might
Darkness rises to the zenith's height

The bells ring all through the night
Panic runs deep, I turn in flight
I run from the shadows, pursuing light
I run like a child, lacking knight

The bells ring all through the night
I turn and face the darkness plight
There I found the courage fight
There I find my inner knight

The bells rang all through the night
Until the sun shown so bright

The bells rang all through the night
Only God knew my might

The bells rang all through the night
As darkness faded out of sight

The bells rang all through the night
(There I stand in victories sight)

Walk Up to Walk Down

Oh Death knock if you may
      but I… I may be out
Let yourself in, have a drink… or three

As I shall not wait for thee
      but quite the other way around
Heaven I will see, yet free will
      and life I will experience first
For my task is not yet complete

When it's time I shall follow
      make your work easy upon your feet
I simply hope that we walk down
      To walk up over your Masters head
Into the Realm where Hope and Desire need not reside
      as all Want is fulfilled

Into the Bath

Into the bath we go now
Into the bath we go
Into the bath we go now
Into the bath we go

With the water running slow now
With the water running slow
With the water running slow now
Into the bath we go

We scrub our feet and wash our face
      Wash our face, wash our face
We scrub our feet and wash our face
      Wash our face, wash our face

Until another takes our place
      Takes our place, takes our place
Until another takes our place
      And we're all in bed sleeping

It's Time for Bed

It's time for bed, it's time to sleep
Begin counting all those sheep
Begin counting as they leap

For the day is done
And the night has come

Fair well, sleep tight
All through the night

Night

The night is young
The night is old
And dawn is almost near
Its time for bed
Its time to sleep
For there's nothing left to fear

Multiple Choice

You know the rule for every test
The answers always C
Unless it's not, then its B
If not C or B, then definitely D
If it can't be all three
Then A's your choice, I do attest
See there's no need to stress
For my strategy certainly is the best

Bored

I told my dad that I was bored
I asked him what to do
He grabbed his hammer and said come aboard
And now I'm holding up sails, but at least I have a view

Yak

There was a yak who liked to yak
Who always yaked out back
Most of the yak the yak did yak
Was all full of jack
Until one day he could not yak
He could not yak any more yak
But the yak did yak
When he did try to yak
But all that came was a big sounding quack

Epigrams

Vegetables
I love my vegetables…
That's why I don't eat them

Pyramids
They said it was so cool…
Why am I so hot

Love
I've always been told love hurts
No thanks

Jumping on Leaves

Jumping on leaves
Seems like such fun
Unless you are the leaves
    Would you get off please
    You surely weigh a ton

Dance

Do you like to dance?
No?! Why not?
What do you mean it's hard?
No, it's not
Let me show you how

You can wave your hands
Like the tall trees
On a windy day
Or sway back and forth
Like the ocean tide

Move your feet like a vogelkop bird
Watch him hop all around
Or try the waggle
It works for the honeybee
No? Still not sure?

Maybe a waggle is too hard
But how about a wiggle
Like a flame
Who can't help but dance
Just watch it go

Or try to write your name
How? With your butt of course!
What do you mean?
No, it's not lame
No, I'm not insane

I'm dancing
And don't look now
But so are you

Float

Grandma sent the float
It's hot enough outside
Now I wish I had a pool
So I could give it a ride

Few are the Ears

The morning wind forever blows
Whispering of life and love
The poem of creation is uninterrupted
From the beginning of time to the future unknown
But few are the ears who hear it
How sad the world has grown

Thc Wind

Who has caught the wind?
I say neither I nor you
But watch the bird in flight
His wings have, it's true

Who has caught the wind?
I say neither you nor I
But what a feeling it would be
To be as a bird and fly

The Man's Jaguar

There was an old man in his car
Who was told to drive a jaguar
But when he looked down
He had quite a frown
And asked "would you like the salad bar"

Skip, Skip, Skip to my Darling

Skip, skip, skip to my darling
As the birds sing off in the farling
Around, around she skips around
Until she's dizzy and falls right down
She falls right down upon the ground

Rain is Falling

The rain is falling, falling, falling down
It's making the ground all muddy and brown
Chloee asks for the sun to chase away the grey
So she can go out to shout and play

The Boy who Dreamed

There was a boy who dreamed a dream
But thought he was not dreaming
Until he woke to the moonlights beam
And his little sister's screaming

My Shadow

It seems I've lost my shadow
Do you know where it may be
I checked the pipes and in the rainbow
I looked in the dog's mouth and on top of the tree
I even yelled into the dark "Hello!"
Maybe in the morning he'll come back to me

Travel

To be able to travel the world is a blessing in countless ways. Traveling will help us along our journey as we seek adventure, as we search for the wildlife of our world, as we encounter the oft times funny and unfamiliar reality of other cultures and customs, as we yearn for the solace and medicine of nature, travel can be the road to take us there. Traveling allows us to get outside of our small bubbles of everyday life. It can help us see the wider world for what it is, helping us recognize our small place in it, but also helping us to connect to the almost 8 billion other human beings on this planet. It is also a chance to broaden our horizons, try new foods, and detach in a way that can help us reach our full potential as human beings living in a world of community. To inspire and light the fires of travel, let's take a tour of the globe.

America the Beautiful

There's no place on Earth
As beautiful as America
There's no place on this planet
With such diversity of scenery

From the rock coasts of the East
The fog of the morn in the crashing of waves
With the beckon of guidance shining from the lighthouse
This is America the beautiful

Then there's the crop fields of the Midwest
Where the breeze plays the corn and the wheat
A song only heard upon American ears
This is America the beautiful

How about the orchards of the South
They grow under the orange harvest moon
As it shines in a sky wide enough to make you dizzy
This is America the beautiful

In the deserts of the Southwest
There lives a serenity as you hear the Indian spirits
Dancing the summer sun away
This is America the beautiful

Up in the Mountain West we can feel the cold
In a forest so thick and snow so white
You would believe you found the mystic beauty of Narnia
This is America the beautiful

How about the grassy plains of the Northeast
Where prairies reign and life slows the hands of time
Under natures pastures of life, animals roam free
This is America the beautiful

We can't forget the sundrenched coast out West
Where beaches and sand are in abundance
There's no better place to view the setting sun over endless water
This is America the beautiful

Of course there is still the paradise of the Southeast
Where the sounds of tropical life float upon the air
Palm trees and cabanas invite relaxation
This is America the beautiful

There's no place on Earth that can offer such a diverse
Beauty of scenery painted across the country's canvas
How beautiful is this land, America
America the beautiful

Land of Opportunity

As true as the eagle soars
As core to seeing Old Glory fly
In America the opportunity is yours
It's simply waiting for those willing to try

Freedom has come at a great cost
For our soldiers have paid the price
In America we ensure their efforts are not lost
By striving for more than just what will suffice

This is the land of U.S.
Hard work and success are always at hand
We fight for the freedom of the oppress
Together as one under God we stand

There is no other country as great as ours
Where the possibilities are endless
Forever we shall remember those stars
And stripes that signify progress

So let's let freedom ring
Forever praise to America, let's sing

The Immigrant

An Immigrant there was, devout in his way
He worked for little pay.
Yet ten percent, he would give
That's the way he was taught to live.
By the ways of the Holy Book
He always gave and never took.
His hands were callused and worn,
His face, beaten and torn,
But none could see
That he was happy, (full of glee).

He looks as if he has traveled
From a far off place, (that has not dazzled).
He's come to work the fields
So that he may bring pride and power to his shields.
For he values the finest things in life
God, his children, and his wife.
But I must stop now
For time will not allow
Me to tell of all his good deed
So I must proceed.

Rooftops

There are rooftops upon rooftops
Some new, some old
Some high, some low
Some brown, some gray, some red
Some shine so bright with reflected sun
Some hide within the shadows comfort grace
Some rooftops are flat and others are pointed
Although all are different, all are the same
A rooftop is a rooftop, accomplishing its task
Protecting those beneath it without a question to ask

Paris Night Song

Come,
Let us wander the streets
Hand and hand, all night.

I love you.

Across the bridge
Along the Seine
By the Eiffel Tower.
With stars and city lights
Shinning down upon
The beauty of you.

Hear the music escape
From inside.

I love you.

Come,
Let us wander the streets
Hand and hand, all night.

Sonnet

Remember when we first met, long ago
I was so young, gently you sought me out
Softly calling to my soul to follow
I remember following with no doubt
You stood by me as I steadily grew
You taught me the joy that comes from the truth
Spending time with you gave me a new view
I'm grateful to have found you in my youth
Even now it's hard for me to discern
How important you are to life's meaning
And what your sacrifice truly did earn
Sacrificial blood of baptisms cleaning
      To learn that my life is not about me
      Is the wisdom that at last set me free

Limerick 1 (Young Girl with a Drum)

There was a young girl with a drum
Who pounded until my head was numb
She drummed all day and night
It was really quite a fright
So I smashed the young girls drum

Limerick 2 (Old Man who ate Fish)

There was an old man who ate fish
For every meal, with every dish
His smell was quite awful
It certainly couldn't be lawful
For this old man to smell like fish

Limerick 3 (Young Kid who ate Crickets)

There was a young kid who ate crickets
And he went around selling tickets
People from all over town
Came to watch him eat them down
This yucky kid who ate crickets

Limerick 4 (Professor of Magic)

There was a professor of magic
Whose story is quite tragic
He taught the students to conjure bread
By mistake their spell cut off his head
This poor professor of magic

'Twas the Night Before Christmas – A Visit from God

'Twas the night before Christmas when all over the earth
Not a creature knew of the miraculous birth
For the inns were full, not a single room to spare
As Mary and Joseph stood in the cold winter's air

Due to Caesar, the world was to be enrolled
Or was it to ensure He was born as foretold
"In Bethlehem the virgin shall bear a son
They shall name him Emmanuel," God's will be done

Freezing and tired from the long journey they came
To the door of the inn with no room as they claim
With pity the inns keeper sent them to the barn
The humble beginnings of God's greatest yarn

In this way our Lord was born, by the warmth of an ox
Swaddled in cloth, in a manger, the pigs feeding box
He lay asleep with his mother all snug and warm
When out of the heavens came music, like a loud winter storm

For this was the day that the star did appear
For this was the day that the Magi jumped with cheer
They knew the time was near, they knew they had to come
Upon camels backs they rode, of where we know not from

The star shone brighter in the sky than any had seen
A beacon creating a path to peace serene
The star still burns today, in a different way
In our hearts the path of the Holy Spirit does lay

In the fields there were shepherds keeping watch this night
Struck with fear as an angel brought God's glory bright
Calming them so he proclaimed the good news
"Jesus is born, Messiah for all not just the Jews"

When he left to heaven, they said we must go
They found Mary and Joseph with the baby so
When they saw what they saw they had to spread the word
All who would listen were amazed at what they heard

Now there lies baby Jesus so small and meek
Yet all the world feels his pull and yearn to seek
His love as innocent as the child new
With chubby hands and that first smile so true

What child is this all wrapped in white
With those delicate eyes that radiate light
This child the ultimate symbol of love
Calling down upon us the wisdom from above

Born into this blessed world for you and I
Born into this confused world to suffer and die
Through this new life so mild, he does bring
Hope and happiness like the bloom of spring

The Magi came as they followed the star
From the east they came, we know not how far
Wise they were to recognize the stars blaze
When they found baby Jesus they gave him holy praise

As they knelt down before him and his mother too
Prostrating themselves before the newborn king they knew
They opened their treasures, gifts for the king they did confer
Precious gold, sweet frankincense, and aromatic myrrh

And this is how it happened, how our savior was born
In a swaddling cloth laying in a manger worn
Angel choirs singing to baby Jesus, Joseph, and Mary his wife
"Merry Christmas to all, and to all a blessed life!"

Jesus Flower

There stood in a desert of sand
Out of place, yet majestic and grand
A flower of white, bright and clear
From its root a spring did appear

All the people of the village came
To see its petals pure as flame
Simply gazing upon its beauty so
Love in their hearts did grow

To the world they preached its story
Hoping to spread its glory
But some began to fear its power
And plotted to uproot this flower at a particular hour

That hour came upon the day of the feast
They came as if searching to kill a beast
When they found the flower unprotected and meek
They took it for granted thinking it was weak

They reached out their hand
And uprooted the flower from the sand
Hoping to destroy its being
Although blind to what they were seeing

What they did not see as they ripped up this flower
Were countless seeds that did begin to shower
From its heart they flowed so free
Into the water these seeds did flee

The wicked believed they had won
But soon the flowers purpose was done
In the barren sand that the wicked wanted, the seeds
                                began to grow and spread
Before long it became a meadow of flowers instead

From this one whose death brought life
With the help of the wind and rain through much strife
The world is now full of flowers so bright
A simple reminder of the fight won that night

Though Jesus did die
His resurrection into the sky
Has brought us endless happiness
These seeds too will grow to something glorious

From death in flower these seeds did come
If planted and watered a new flower will grow in the sun
So from life to death to life again
The same shall come to those who follow Jesus, amen!

Terracotta Army

In a land of extremes
Bitter cold when the sun is low
Scathing hot when the sun is high
Amidst the pomegranate fruits of heaven

There lies an army, waiting

Defenders of the Emperor
Each warrior unique in himself
Yet apart of the uniformity of repetition
To see the sea of heads all in a line

For each with their role and responsibility
To Qin Shi Huangdi in the afterlife

China

The land, separated by the great wall
It is a marvel to see in peace
Deep in the misty mountains
Two types of wisdom can be found
One protected by monks
Practicing kung fu and Zen meditation
The other is found in the mind of the panda
As she munches on fresh bamboo

Great Wall (Zen Poem)

The stones of gray and gold
Next to the green tree so old
With setting sun orange in the sky
The beauty of China

Zhangjiajie (Zen Poem)

Tall spires of quartz-sandstone
Dressed in the deep green of dense forest
Fog hides the canyon floor
Creating mystery and calm
Water falls from the sky above
Washing all clean
Transports all to another world

Leshan Buddha (Zen Poem)

The cleansing water flows at his feet
He is robed in emerald green trees
Sitting on a throne of red sandstone
Like the confluence of the river below
He teaches confluence of reality and illusion
Come marvel at the experience of happiness
As Maitreya brings peace to the world

Witches Chair

There's a spot in Ireland
On a hill high and green
The legend says a witch lived here
Her stone throne can still be seen
It's said if you sit on her chair
And in earnest you ask a wish
If she likes you and thinks it fair
Then your wish may come true
When we went to her chair
Under the torrents of rain
My wife sat down and asked
For the sunshine instead
Immediately, the rain stopped
And the sun came out and shown
But as soon as we left that little hill
The rain began again
I can't explain it
But this story is true
I don't know what to say
The witch seemed to like us
Upon this our lucky Irish day

Fairy Tree

Have you ever seen a fairy tree?
I have once
Driving down a little lane
In the green hills of Ireland
It stood tall between the road
All covered in ribbons and bows
I can't explain why
But this tree is special
Its magic made me happy
Just to see its beauty
Surrounded by beauty
Next to my beauty

Ireland in Spring

Its early in the spring
Winters all done
Fairies flutter upon the wing
Spring, it's time for leprechaun fun

The flowers are in blooms
And the druids begin to sing
In the deep-water something booms
What joy there is this Irish spring

Mountain Haiku

In misty mountains
They like to play hide n' seek
When found brings peace

Sun (Zen Poem)

Watching the sun over the sea
Rises with a flood of red and orange

Working when the sun is over head
Its warmth gives life to the earth

Contemplating the sun as it sets over the hills
He promises to come back tomorrow

Brazil

The air is filled with the sounds
Of notes that float upon the tropical wind
As samba and bossa nova comes from the towns
It will put you in the right state of mind

Along the jungles so fresh and green
An abundance of wildlife flourishes here
Floating through the flooded forest is so serene
The allure will never be more clear

The colors of the macaws and birds
The majesty of the jaguars
Seeing such a scene will leave you with no words
It's like witnessing the birth of a star

The anteaters and sloths so stealth
Can be hard to find, what a game
But when you find them its such wealth
You won't regret you came

The night sky is second to none
In the dark of the jungle to see
The black sky covered with billions of glittering suns
To view the southern cross and the milky way will bring you to your knees

The world's most beautiful and largest waterfall
And some of the most spectacular and pristine beaches
For the outdoor enthusiast, Brazil has it all
Just listen to the land as it preaches

Christ the Redeemer and Carnival
Iguaçu Falls and the Amazon
Pantanal and islands so tropical
I hear you calling, I feel so drawn

Then there's still the flavors and spice
Churrasco and brigadeiro so savory and sweet
Perfected culinary skill so precise
I can hardly wait to eat

But what makes this country so great
Are its people so beautiful and full of bliss
They take what they are given, grabbing ahold of fate
This is a country I continually miss

For there is beauty and majesty in this unique landscape
It is full of adventure, expectation, and thrill
It's the type of place and experience that will change your life's shape
Full of friends and food this exceptional place called Brazil

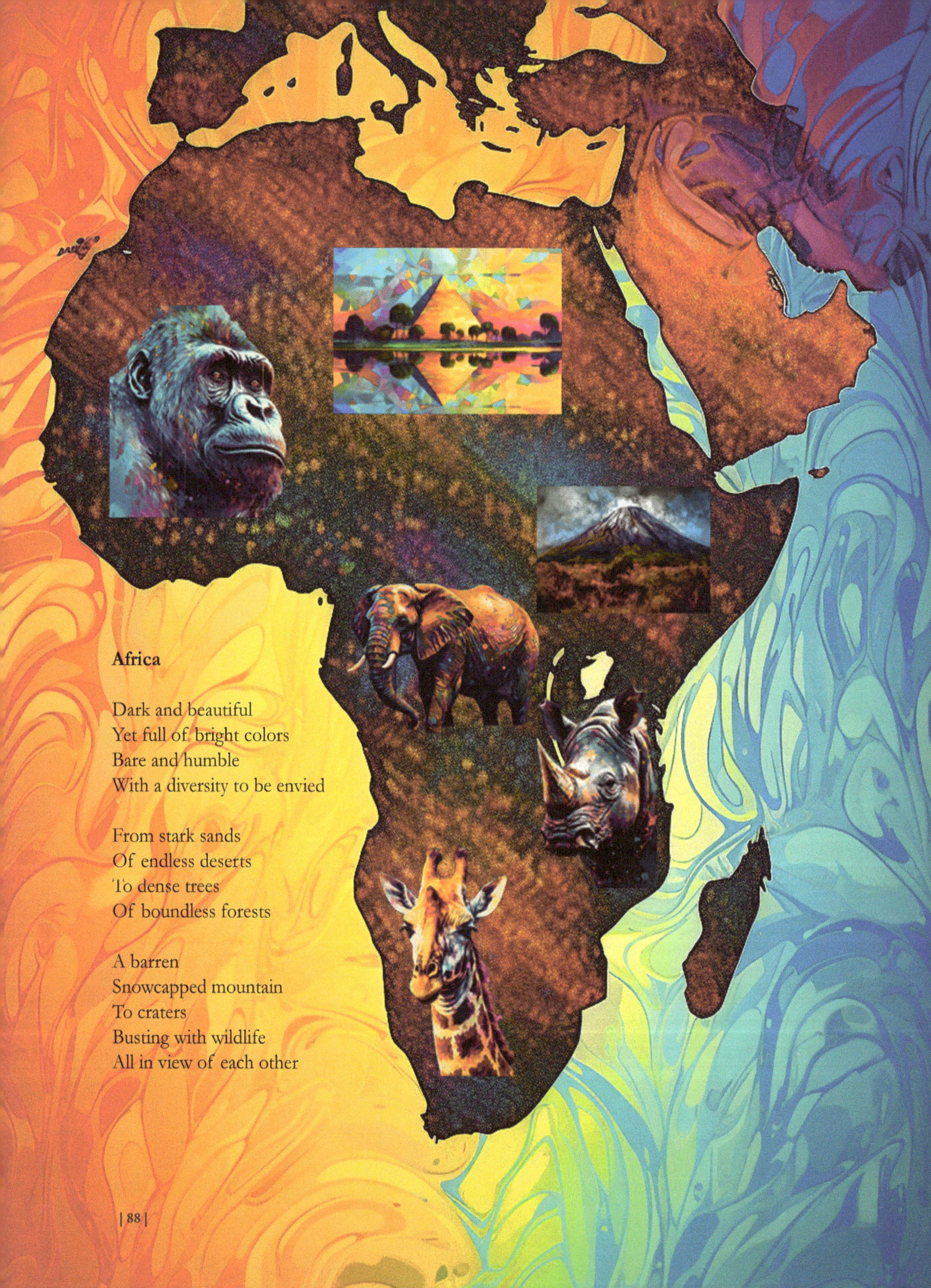

Africa

Dark and beautiful
Yet full of bright colors
Bare and humble
With a diversity to be envied

From stark sands
Of endless deserts
To dense trees
Of boundless forests

A barren
Snowcapped mountain
To craters
Busting with wildlife
All in view of each other

From drought driven famine
To floods
From hidden, seemingly endless
Rain

Abject poverty
Yet you sing
With a smile
And a joy
That is contagious

A land that holds
Unknown and untapped potential
That grows
In your fertile soil

Among the
Garden of creation
It's still truly
A paradise on Earth

The Cross

In a desert, away from everything
I grew in the dirt of a holy land
I was watered by the tears of the afflicted
In the middle of nowhere full of sand

The center of the universe, I am
My seed was from the heavens on high
Like a foreign object familiar yet unknown
On this small hill I stood swaying to the winds lullaby

With a view of all the land below
The hill of my birth… (on a hill I shall die)
Many came to gaze upon me in this barren country
This miraculous tree that grew from a field so dry

My trunk was thick and sturdy
My branches nimble and strong
The children loved to come to me
To play…and swing… and to find respite from the sun's oppressive throng

At last I reached my age of maturity
It was my time to bear much fruit
Yet at this moment, in this season of renewal
They came with saw and axe to cut me down to the root

Slowly, they surveyed my stature, slowly their hearts grew in fear
But they would not stop, they would not flee
Even though they knew to cut me down was going to be a chore
Encouraged by the people, the poachers approached with glee

They always relished a challenge
They became intoxicated with the thud of the first blow
They always looked towards destruction
The axe struck hard, leaving a gash in my bark, what woe

But my wood is hard and resilient
However, this did not hinder their lust
Hack after hack after hack they struck
Digging deeper and deeper and deeper with each thrust

With each strike they cut further and further and further
Into my life's rings the cut became deep
With ropes and saw they pulled me to the ground
No longer standing, they finally had what they came to reap

Just as I thought the worst was over, it began anew
With hatchets they struck and they scrouged, cutting away all they could
Sculpting…shaping… mangling my figure
Until I lay exposed with arms wide open like dead wood

Then they dragged me through the streets of town
And pulled me to the top of the hill
There they laid a man across my beaten and broken body
They forced him upon my disfigured form with his arms outspread and still

The man did not weigh much
For he was already almost dead
We shuttered and shook when they drove the nails through us
Stripped bare we were soaked in his blood so red

I could feel it beginning to absorb into my pores
Pound after pound after pound they drove three enormous nails, each with a thud
Then they raised us up… yes, they raised us up upon the hill
I was at once taken back to when I began to grow in that sacred mud

Somehow in all the pain and agony of the axe
Somehow in all the hacking and the driving of nails
Somehow amidst all the wailing, jeering, and chaos of the scene
Peace came to me, like a calm cool breeze catches the sails

The pain was no more
My purpose had been fulfilled
Standing… carrying all the sin of the world
We were crucified with such skill

I was finally home again
Just a simple wooden cross, a small tree upon a hill
Yet… I feel that all has changed
Because of his surrendering will

In Memoriam: The Fallen Man

I vividly see the shining beast
      Coming over the sand along the East
      With heat and wind does dawn call out
Soldier of the West, march on to your song and shout

For your work here is over, yet just begun
      Over the hill and under the tree your shun
      They wait for thee in anticipation to show
Fast approach a car of dust, in an instant it will blow

O how I love, adore your courage
      And hoped for your return
But vain are hope and dreams! For this the end your voyage
      Death's grip has ripped you from your turn
      Only to place you in his urn

Santa Claus

Santa Clause is a jolly old man
Who's name is also Saint Nick
And from America, to Germany, and Japan
He travels in his sleigh so quick
House to house, to all the good girls and boys
He goes passing out such lovely trinkets and toys

Passing By

Here I stand, upon a road which is not mine
I was passing through I hope they will not mind
For I have stolen a glimmer of their light to rest my blinded eyes
For I have borrowed a smidge of their smell of din to quench my frosted nose
For I have taken their joy of the sight of the steed to warm my heart
All this standing on a snow filled empty road
Unknown to them… unknown to me
Simple fuel to keep my legs moving forward
As I am simply passing by

I Say Goodbye

Its time to say goodbye
Even though we just said hello so shy
We now board our planes to fly
I look back, with memories and sigh

We said hello and now goodbye
Friendships made without a try
Running on adrenaline, emotions high
With eyes of rain, ready to cry

Goodbye is all there is to say goodbye
My head is full of questions why
When I write, please reply
I look away with tears of eye

Goodbye farewell I say to you
Let the memories help us through
For this day would come, we knew
Fight off the sadness, don't be blue

For we are friends for life, this is true
In touch we stay, until our presence renew
My goodbye is drawn and overdue
With this I bid you a great adieu

Wildlife

Spending time with wildlife is a privilege and an opportunity for the truly enlightened to learn about the truths of life. As humans we have been given the honor of stewards to govern the lesser beast. This authority was given to us by none other than God Himself and therefore requires our great attention. We should seek to uphold our duty as stewards of these animals in protecting them and the habitats they live in. I promise those who do work to protect these creatures and habitats will find great compensation and reward. They will begin to truly appreciate the beauty and variety of life that exists on this small yet unique and beautiful planet we call Earth. If you're ready, I would love to introduce you to some of my most precious friends.

The Wolf Hunt

In the Lamar Valley
Of Yellowstone Park
Theres a pack of wolves
That I saw just after dark

They hunted for big game
All seven of them together
Looking for a bison
Even in this weather

They found an old bull
On a plateau just above the ravine
So, the wolves saunter on over
To evaluate the scene

They surrounded this bull bison
All seven to one
Squaring up their chances
Seeing if he would run

Then the alpha female
Squats for the attack
Head to head they go
Skull to skull I heard the smack

As the bull bison watches
The wolf staggers back
With a splitting headache, I'm sure
She looks to her pack

Who decides it's too much work
To take down this old bull
Back to the forest they went
Without even a morsel full

Warning

I stood in the land of the bison
The supposed grasslands of the north
The beauty of the Dakotas is unique
Yet still just a dusty shadow
Of what it used to be
It was a paradise of fauna
Wolves and coyote used to roam free
Among large herds of pronghorn, big horn sheep, and elk
All alongside the enormous herds of bison
The native man lived in, an American Paradise
The Serengeti of the West
But now it's a desert plain full of dirt
The grass is gone, the animals too
They call it Badlands, beautiful but not the same
Oh to have seen it in its past glory and splendor
Now it's just a reminder and a warning
We must protect and preserve
Or we too will perish

The Jaguar

So stealthy, so mighty, so majestic
The queen of the South American jungle
The power of your jaw
The fearlessness of your stalk
A cat with no fear of the water
These are only matched by
The calm of your presence
The serenity in your eyes
There is no anger, no evil to be found
Just a love and contentment of life
A confidence of knowing your power
Without any temptation to abuse it
Yet the spots of your fur
Betray your royal status none the less
How privileged I am, to have seen you
To have watched you
To have spent so many hours in the purity of the jungle with you
To have become friends, even though we shall never see each other again
You I will never forget, your beauty I will forever remember
The control and love which you have mastered, I will mimic
Your love for the simplicity of life
I will take as my example and love for simplicity of life too

The Blue and Yellow Macaw

I was floating… down the mighty river
Through the flooded forest… of the Amazon jungle
I listened… to the calming sound
Of beautiful
When I caught… just a glimpse
Of a flying rainbow
It so gracefully… yet swiftly flew
From one tree… to another
We paddled to see… we strained… we looked
Finally… we saw
Against the green canopy… of the world's greatest rainforest
The world's most beautiful… blue and yellow macaw
He had a small… green patch that he wore… like a crown
The blue of his cape… was so bright
It made the bright blue sky… look pale and gray
In comparison to its brilliance
The yellow of its breast… shone like the sun
Simply warming my heart
With just a moment… to gaze
In just a fleeting breath… to appreciate
He was gone
But his flash of light
This flying rainbow
Will stay with me forever

The Silent Pond

There was a silent little pond
In the middle of a wood
Where the frogs splashed
And the toads croaked all day

I sat by a silent little pond
Hidden in the forest
Where the mockingbirds sang
Backed by a chorus of crickets

I contemplated a silent little pond
Nestled among the hills
As the wind rustled the leaves
And the trees creaked hello

In the middle of the wood
Hidden in the forest
Nestled among the hills
There was a silent…. little pond

Noah's Ark

There was a man named Noah
　　Who built a big ol' ark
God instructed him to build it
　　And hide it in the dark

When the sky grew gloomy
　　God came to say
Take all the animals two by two
　　And hide them all away

Doing what he was told
　　To all the animals he did call
And two by two they came
　　'Til the ark was full and rain began to fall

Then one day, unannounced
　　The sun began to shine
And off the ark they all came
　　In one single file line

Silly Snail

There was a silly slimy snail see
Who sailed the serendipitous sea.
But when this small silly slimy snail
Sailed back upon the slippery sea,
His shell had slipped away spontaneously.
What's this silly slimy snail to do
Without a sparkling shelter of a shell?
Be a simple slug sitting on the shore?
Wait, he sees in the sea his shiny shell
Slowly slinking upon the shallow shore.
The slimy snail sees it show itself
Sitting on the sea at seven past six
So, silly snail's a snail for sure
Slowly sailing the sea you see again.
There is a silly slimy snail see
Who's certainly sailing his shell ship on
The sensationally serendipitous sea

Snail

Who would have known that a snail could be so interestingly complex?
As he hides in a shell not so convex
Only a brilliant mathematician, the great Fibonacci
And the simpleness of a child, the innocent Caylee
Two perspectives as wide-apart as can be, if comparing
Majestic spiral galaxy to this garden snail my daughters carrying
Yet both mysteries, linked, discovered in due time
How uniquely clever is this daughter of mine
One plus one is two plus one is three plus two is five plus three is eight
Do you understand, do you have it all straight?
Oh, never mind. I guess its beauty is only recognized by mathematically genius men
And unpresumptuous pure minded children

Birds of Love

Like the raven in the night
Silhouetted against the glow of the full harvest moon
You bring chills to my soul

Like the flight of the blue bird
Over the midday summer sun
You bring warmth to my heart

Like the song of the nightingale
On the dew of a spring morning
You bring joy to my life

A Bird in the Window

There was a bird in the window
Like the wind from left to right it flew

Black as the night
Yet quick as light

The joys of nature are seen
Through this window so clean

Monkey

Monkey! Monkey! Of the trees
Joy is your laughter

With arms to dangle and feet as hands
Tail to tail swinging, all day playing
Sadness is never known to thee

For responsibility and law escapes you
Always living in the given moment makes you

Lioness

I heard that lion roar
So deep and low in her throat
It was quiet but confident

In my soul I felt that roar
Reverberating down my spine
It left me with awe and wonder

How subtle she can be
Hiding behind our jeep
Watching her prey

The Eagle

Majestically free, head of white
It's rare to catch a glimpse or sight
Above the trees, over the lake in flight

High in crags of mountain walls
You're thrown sits echoing your calls
In our breast a pride upon your image recalls

Gorilla

Gorilla! Gorilla! Of the forest
Ferocious is your roar

With the strength of your might
And fangs as strong as the lion
It is terror to see your anger

How advanced must be your mind
To only kill in battle

Panther

Panther! Panther! Of the night
Silent fear is brought by your sight

With black spots on black fur of silk
Stalking the night with the glow of invisible eyes
Wisdom resides in your council

How calming is your temperament
Yet your bite feared by all the world

Giraffe

Giraffe! Giraffe! Of Africa
Peace is your silence

With your long flowing legs and neck
And your sticky black tongue
It is jest to see your young walk

How full must your head be with thought
As you make not a peep to the world

Tiger Hunt

He's a master of camouflage
      You think you saw him
      But maybe not
He plays with your mind
      Like an animal mirage

His bite is fierce
His claws are sharp
      Worst yet he's as silent
      As a night on the moon
As he waits for his prey to pierce

Orange and black
Like fire in the night
Determination in his eyes
      And a hungry growl in his stomach
      Just looking for a snack

So beware of the tiger cat
      He may just get what's under your hat

Alone (Sadness of the Rhino)

In the African bush
I stand alone
In the quiet of the day
I eat alone

With dark grey clouds overhead
In solitude, I'm alone
When the rain falls
In the flood I drink alone

It's hard to hide
Even when I'm all alone

They push me to the brink
Extinction won't leave me alone
Their search for me is relentless
As they hope to find me alone

Poachers are always in pursuit
To get my horn alone
It's a hard life
Being alone

But I wish they would
Just leave me alone

Baby Elephant

Do you know what cute is?
    It is to see a baby elephant
Do you know what fun is?
    To watch as she plays in the mud
Do you know what it means to test the limits?
    The baby elephant does as she sprays the others
Do you know what joy is?
    To watch her chase a warthog away from the watering hole

Little Big Ears

The smallest big ears I ever saw
Were on a baby elephant at the elephant spa

She played in the water, she played in the mud
Chasing a warthog, she fell with a thud

So cute this little elephant was, what fun
To watch her little legs move, to watch her run

If enjoyment of life was her goal
Then this little elephant found it at her little watering hole

Panda and Balloon

On a wooden bench
A panda and a balloon
Brings joy to my heart

Panda Haiku

The white and black bear
Eating bamboo is endangered
We must save panda

From Me to You

This last section of poems is dedicated first to my three beautiful daughters, Chloee, Caylee, and Carlee. Many of these poems were written for them. I also included poems written for other family members as well as poems that can be a reminder of things I hope my girls will have learned from me about life and what is truly important, such as about God and family. Many of these poems are deeply personal and I hope you get a sense of the love that I tried to infuse into these poems as I struggled to capture things that cannot be put into words. Without further ado, these poems are from me to you.

Only Those

Only those who believe
    can see the future.
Only those who strive
    will reach their goals.
Only those who care
    can make a change.
Only those who take action
    can accomplish.
Only those who try
    will grow.
Only those who work
    can succeed.

Dream Your Dreams

Dream your dreams as you may
Yet nothing they shall become
If always in your head they stay

I prefer to live reality
Where life and hope may become
As beautiful as a symphonic melody

It's here that all my efforts I shall aim
Where dreams and reality become the same
It's here that all my happiness came

Growing Tree

You're like a seed we planted years ago
Time has passed, some fast, some slow
From this seed came a small plant so cute
Like a little baby Groot
You ran and smiled and grew so fast
We knew this stage would never last
As our first we learned along the way
Simply enjoying life day by day
With each day you bring us something new
How much I love you through and through
Not yet fully grown, but your trunk and leaves are strong
I know you'll be leaving in not too long
But always remember who watered you so
Oh, how hard it is to let you go
But not so fast, that time has not yet come
We get to keep you a little longer some
So, we will keep pruning and tending you each year
As we cultivate and watch the fruit appear

Children Don't See…

Children don't see race
Just a beautiful face
Children don't see different colored skin
They only know the person within

He doesn't know she's black
Just that she wants to share her snack
She doesn't know he's white
Just that they like to fly his kite

Society hasn't indoctrinated them yet
To see differences as a threat
Oh what I wouldn't do
To show them what society teaches is just not true

To teach them that grown-ups are wrong
That the differences really make us strong
I wish children would stick to their way
And together, go out and play

Eyes a Mirror

The thought of having this child of mine
    A world changing, I face it with fear
For a new life will be here clinging by my side
    Looking into her eyes, my eyes a mirror

For life's so precious and careless as she
    So young, so wise, so pure she laughs
In this scary world she faces with me
    Oh how I wish for her faith secure

For I love her with all my heart
I loved her first, from the start

Graduation

I look to the past
And think how time has blown by so fast
I think of those events sublime
And all the wonderful pastime
I think of the times I've had
Whether good or bad
I've spent the last thirteen years in this familiar place
Now graduation has caused me to trace
The many years I've spent in school
Of those times that I've felt cool
And those I've played the fool
I think of my teachers
Those who were mentors
Of knowledge and life
Then I think of those teachers
Who caused much eager toil and strife
I think of my friends
Those who said they'll love me to all ends
I think of all the good times I had with them
Listening to music, playing sports, and causing mayhem
Or just hanging' out
Doing calculus till we wanted to shout
Yes, I think of the good times I've had
But now it's all about to change
It's time to exchange
The greatly dreaded good-bye's
As all of the emotions arise
For none like to depart
From their closest friends, that have been there from the start
But it's time to move on
This chapter in my life is about to be gone
But the key, is to stay strong
Because before long
A new chapter is to begin
That brings the unknown, new experiences, and changes from within
It is important to look to the future that lies therein
But I will never forget what has been

Your Day

The transition point has come
Through the struggles of the past
Although the end for some
This is definitely not your last

We're so proud of the path you set
Our support you have indeed
Our expectations you've always met
Count on us in good times and in need

Challenging life you go on
But stop to enjoy your day
For success will bring another dawn
And there are many on their way

What's a Valentine

What's a heart? Anything you want it to be
A silly little love bug with googly eyes
Maybe the wings of a butterfly, look how it flies
It could be anything your imagination can see

What's love? How you feel, all you do
A hug in my arms so warm and tight
The way we have fun with all our might
Or a kiss goodnight from me to you

What's a valentine? A piece of paper with a lyrical rhyme
Maybe in a way it could be so
But more a symbol of my love for you, you know
A love that we share for all time

So that's what it is, a heart, my love, my valentine
So will you promise to always be mine?

Valentine Haiku

On this day of love
Your bright smile and laughter
Is my Valentine

On Birds Wings

On birds wings you have begun to fly
Soaring towards the white clouds of the sky
It seems not long ago you were an eaglet
Helpless and young not ready for the world quite yet

Now however, it is a sight to see you soar
As you test and try and explore
Pressing the limits of what you can do
Experiencing the world from such heights, what a view

I will always be here at the nest
Watching, waiting, just knowing I'm blessed
To have such a bird who rises above the rest
Who doesn't back down, even when she's pressed

With my love like wind in your wings carrying you up like a kite
You keep soaring to new height

Being Oneself

Label not yourself or others
For labels only distort that which makes each of us unique

Focus not on successes and failures
For competition and jealousy are the tools of Satan

Focus not on material substance
For this is how misers and thieves come to be

Style is no substitute for substance
So let there be no definition of action

For all are unique and beneficial
So let one's true self shine without restraint

Thinking of My Babies

Baby smiles
Baby cries
Babies fast asleep
The joy of past
The hope of future
These memories I will keep

What are Light?

What are light? sea-foam and laughter
What are long? grief and ever after
What are strong? ants and love
What are pure? a child's smile and God above

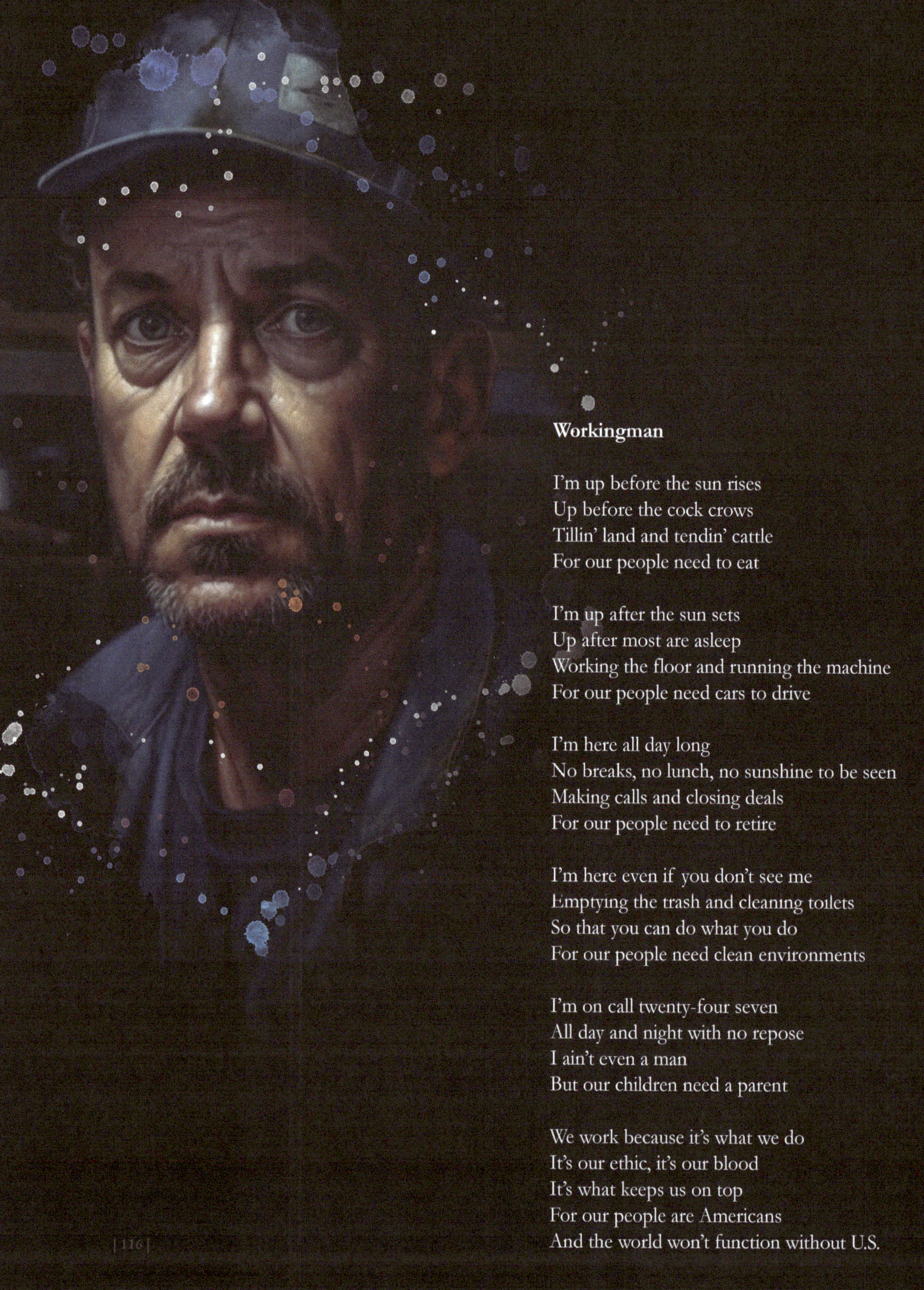

Workingman

I'm up before the sun rises
Up before the cock crows
Tillin' land and tendin' cattle
For our people need to eat

I'm up after the sun sets
Up after most are asleep
Working the floor and running the machine
For our people need cars to drive

I'm here all day long
No breaks, no lunch, no sunshine to be seen
Making calls and closing deals
For our people need to retire

I'm here even if you don't see me
Emptying the trash and cleaning toilets
So that you can do what you do
For our people need clean environments

I'm on call twenty-four seven
All day and night with no repose
I ain't even a man
But our children need a parent

We work because it's what we do
It's our ethic, it's our blood
It's what keeps us on top
For our people are Americans
And the world won't function without U.S.

Darkness of the Soul

God's love hides in the darkness of the soul
Waiting patiently to be freed
Yet most walk by in a hurry and fear of the night
Missing their chance to capture His eternal light

Like the blind staring into the sun
Like the deaf with the trumpets of Triumph blast in their ear
Like the mute whose scream reaches the depths of their soul
Ignorance is not bliss but the blessing of Lucifer upon your head

Beware… for his light has been snuffed
You shall not find God there
In his light you are blind and vulnerable, impressionable you become
Clothe yourself in His darkness; take comfort you may still escape

If…

If the earth could be brighter
By the laughter in your eye's
Day would forever shine

If the cold could be warmed
By the love in your hug
We would all live in a tropical forest

If people could be made better
By giving them presents
Then your presence alone would be more than enough

There's no little girl with more joy
Than you can bring to me
My world is brighter, warmer, and better because of you

Living Story

A book in hand
Is better than a book on the shelf
A story told
Is better than a story lost

Just the same, a love that's shared
Is better than a love left alone
So every day I thank God
For you are your mother and my shared love

Like a good book can give you so much
Adventure and fear, excitement and relief
Laughter and tears, admiration and joy
Loving you is like this too.

There's always a little fear in every adventure taken
From this comes courage, hope, and excitement
Along the way there is laughter and tears
But in the end there's joy and endless admiration

A real life story that is beyond compare
To anything that could be written
I devour the days like perfect chapters
Always holding with baited breath to see what happens

But this I know for sure
You never disappoint and never cease to amaze
You are a treasure that I am undeserving to have
Yet so grateful for the gift all the more

A gift you are, and gifted so
There's no other person more like me than you
A story read can be great
But your story lived has been life changing

There's not a single Chloee in the whole world
That I love more than you
Oh, how much I love you

You're Like a Rare Book

You're like a rare book
Just begging to be read
You hold stories of adventures took
Or little fairytales enjoyed before bed

Your smile is like a rhythmic poem about a flower
Your eyes bring the wisdom like a May shower
But you can be serious too
Like a mystery that you slowly step through

Like all good books, I love to sit with you by the fire
Snuggle up and look at you as I truly admire
Most of all you are the promise that every book holds
And I love to watch you as your story unfolds

Journey in a Book

I open this secret place
That only I can see
Although I am sitting here to the outside view it's me
But in my head I am a million miles away
Immersed in the life and world of another day
It may have been far, or not, in the past
Or out into the future untamed and vast
It might be a place and time so true
Or more often than not in the imagination magical portal I walked through
I can curl up in a chair, on my bed, or in the car
Away I go who knows how far
There is no limit to what we can see
If you would only pick up a book with me
Together we journey down the road
As we watch the infinite explode
Like a good book I see how you develop and grow
With excitement and anticipation to see how it all ends, only God will know
But it's a great journey along the way
I will continue to enjoy each page and each day
As I watch the effects of time
Marching through each valentine
It tells your story from year to year
Oh how much I love you I hope it's clear

Ducky Water Blue

My love for you is endless bound
I'm filled with love by just the smallest of sound
Of the pitter patter of your little feet
Or the smile upon your face when I give a cookie sweet
How I cherish the joy in your eye
When there's a "doggie!" that you spy
Like a duck who yearns for the water blue
That's how much love I love for you

The Middle

Sometimes it's hard
Being in the middle
But most of the time it's great

There's peanut butter between the bread
And the ice cream between two cookies
The middle is what brings the smile

The best part of a book
Is the story and adventure
That's found between the front and back covers

There's being the younger
While also being the older
You are the best of both worlds

Many amazing things
Come in the middle
Like you and me

One of my favorite things
I've found in the middle
Is you in a hug between mom and me

Sometimes it's hard
Being in the middle
But most of the time it's great

A Girl Like You

The world needs more girls like you
Strong willed and confident
Unassuming and caring
True to herself and her purpose

My world needs a girl like you
To remind me of the future we have
And to help me remember the past
You and me, we are two cut from the same cloth

I love that you are you
I love that you don't let anyone
Change you and that you
Change for no one

You bring me hope
You make me smile
Because I am you
And you are me

The world needs more girls like you
My world needs a girl like you

Journey

Adventure awaits and memories made
That sums up our lives so far
We've seen and done so much
The two of us together

We've stood upon mountain tops
Looking over fields of ice millions of years old
We've swam in oceans so clear and warm
Watching manta rays glide through the silky waters

We've created a home that welcomes us back when we've been gone
We're raising three beautiful and strong daughters
We've met the challenges of life head on
And by the grace of God made it through so far

Yet with all we have done, more than many do in a lifetime
There is still so many more adventure out there
Greater wonders of life lie ahead
Daughter's to marry and grandkids horizons to expand

There are still islands to hike
Ruins to explore and animals to observe
Cities to experience and plays to enjoy
Endless variety of cuisine to savor

But even with all the splendor that lies ahead
All the beauty this world still has to offer
All the adventure that still awaits
I am most excited to do this journey with you

As you make the beauty of the world more majestic
You make the challenges more bearable
You make the flavors more savory
And you make my life more vibrant

Anticipating the next adventure with you brings me excitement
Journeying through this life with you is my joy
Making memories with you is my love

Each and All Because of You

All truth, all goodness, all beauty in you
Continues to brighten each day anew
Each breath, each smile, each twinkle in your eye
Continues to tell the story of you and I

Each hug, each kiss, each lovers embrace
Is but the radiance of God's great grace
You, with me, together through all time
Is but a poem in life's perfect rhyme

Waking, dreaming, souls never apart
All roads from you lead straight to my heart
All that I am, my joy, my life
Oh how I love you my amazing and beautiful wife

American History

Diversity
Such a loaded term
To all, some connotation
Positive or negative
It could be

Melting pot
It's our story
Whether we like it
Or not
It's just the way it goes
the way it went

Convergence
It's what America is
All of history and culture stops here
Just check the logs
Every country is represented here

Promise
To some the ultimate hope
Others simply waiting to be broken
It's possibility
That's U.S.

Imagination

There is no limit to where you go
How I love to watch your mind glow
Like your father you're all in
Always keep this fire burning from within
Your creativity gives me wonder
Like the beauty of a desert summer storm, all lighting and thunder

I love to see all your creations
Even if I don't always get their applications
But most of all I love to see your smile when you show them to me
How light it makes you, totally free
Letting your imagination paint all you do
There's no doubt in your gifts I see you
And that I will treasure for all time
Especially knowing you're all mine

If I had to confesstest
I love you extra most bestest

Brother

My first memory is of me
Looking through the window at the age of three
Waiting for my best friend to return
From school, his company I did yearn

From that day on he's been my compass
My northern star or guide in my looking glass
I've always looked up to him, always wanting him around
Even when I became taller than him, I looked up when looking down

He's shown me kindness and frustration
He's put me at risk but given endless protection
He's my Google when it comes to fixing anything
He's my soldier who defended our right to let freedom ring

There's no other more selfless
Willing to open his home to the distress
Would give up the shirt on his back
If it meant another could live without lack

From music to hobbies and the clothes I wore
He's influenced my life all the way to my core
There's nothing I can't ask of him that he wouldn't do
Because we're family and that's the standard he holds himself to

From the beginning of life to the end
By my side forever he'll be my friend
In blood and in love we are bound
A better brother will never be found

So as he is to me, I strive for the same in his eye
Through all of life, I'm with him, my brother, to the day we die
Forever his love I'll rely
My endless support he'll always have by and by

I am me because of you

You gave me strength and endurance
Like the waves that crash upon the shore
Yet you taught me compassion for others
So I can whisper comfort like the ocean breeze

I am me because of you

I have knowledge of right and wrong
So I can fly like a bird over the sea
With this you also taught me responsibility
So I can shine like a lighthouse on stormy nights

I am me because of you

Most of all you gave me love, in abundance
Which is why I have so much love to share
You are my joy and I will always love you
As you and I shimmer like the rising sun

I am me because of you
This we both know is true

Illustrations were imagined by Justin A Guerra, rendered in Midjourney, and post processed in Adobe Photoshop.

First Edition 2023

Print ISBN   978-1-0881-1348-6
E book ISBN 978-1-0881-1356-1